LOTUS

HIBISCUS

TORCH GINGER

PHILODENDRON

NANA HONUA

GEORGIA IN HAWAII

When Georgia O'Keeffe Painted What She Pleased

By Amy Novesky • Illustrated by Yuyi Morales

HARCOURT CHILDREN'S BOOKS

Houghton Mifflin Harcourt   Boston   New York   2012

To Georgia and the island of Kauai,
to my mom and dad, Bonny and Roger,
and to Elsie, with a flower behind her ear. —— A.N.

To Jim, Maria, Karen, Gianna, and Lynn —— the Revisionaries.
And to Sam, my editor and forever one of us. —— Y.M.

After five days at sea, Georgia O'Keeffe arrived on a green island in the middle of the Pacific Ocean. She was greeted with silver coins and leis of plumeria, wild ginger, and crown flower.

Aloha, Georgia!

It was February 1939, and the Hawaiian Pineapple Company had invited the famous artist to tour Hawaii. They wanted her to create two paintings to promote the delights of pineapple juice.

Georgia visited the pineapple fields soon after her arrival on the island of Oahu. She found the sharp and silvery fruit quite strange and beautiful. She wanted to live nearby so she could study it up close.

But the Pineapple Company would not let her. Only workers lived near the fields, they said. Georgia protested that she was a worker too and could live wherever she wanted. The company refused to allow it.

Instead, they presented her with a pineapple. Georgia was
disgusted. She did not want to paint the fruit now that it had been
picked. And she would not let anyone tell her what to paint.

Despite the pineapple trouble, Georgia started her tour. She flew to the island of Maui. There she stayed on an old sugar plantation at the edge of a rainforest and carried a paper umbrella when it rained. In a borrowed banana wagon, she drove the tightly winding mountain roads. Georgia went where she wanted, when she wanted.

And Georgia painted!

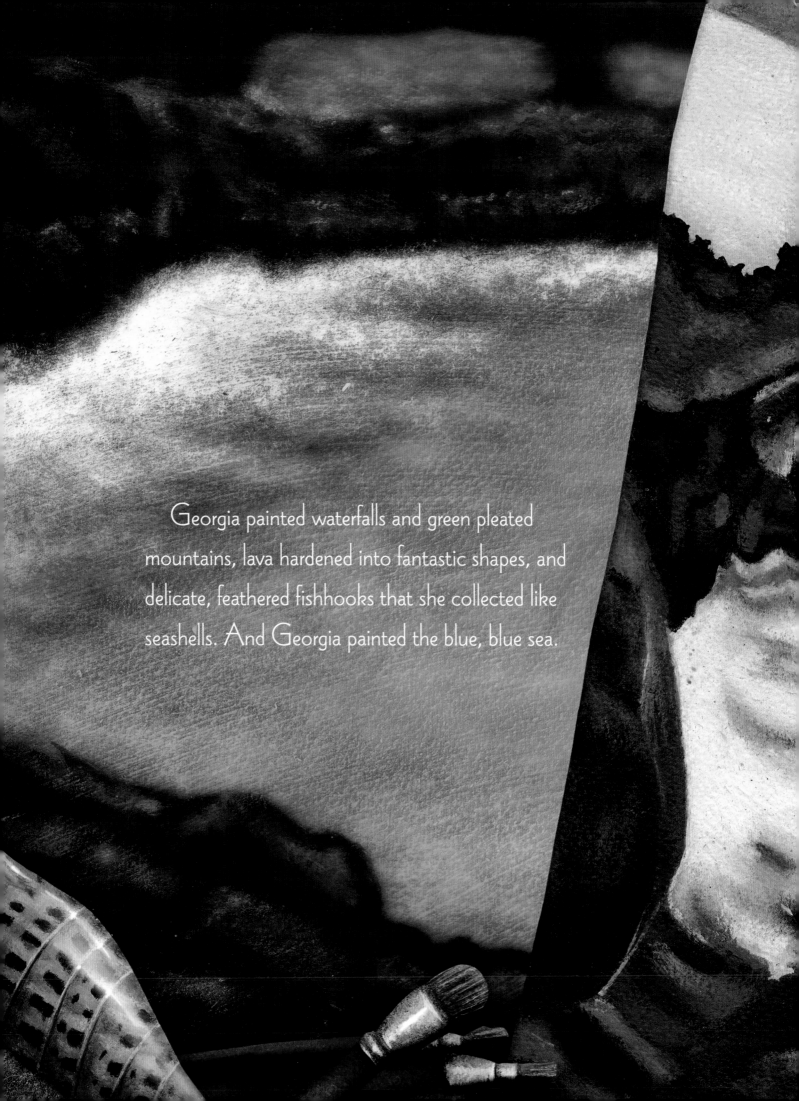

Georgia painted waterfalls and green pleated mountains, lava hardened into fantastic shapes, and delicate, feathered fishhooks that she collected like seashells. And Georgia painted the blue, blue sea.

Next she traveled by steamer to the big island of Hawaii, where she admired volcanoes that rose thousands of feet into the sky. She walked on black sand beaches reached only by boat and studied a rare piece of red coral. She met the local cattle ranchers, or *paniolo*. These Hawaiian cowboys showed her their gardens

And Georgia painted flowers!
Bird of paradise and philodendron, foot-long heliconia and fragrant
plumeria, torch ginger and silver cup, lotus and hibiscus.
She painted a *nana honua* that she'd picked by the side of
the road. It reminded Georgia of her favorite desert flower, the
jimsonweed.

In Kauai, her last stop, Georgia visited with local artists. She stayed at the seaside home of a former Hawaiian queen near Koloa, a small mill town surrounded by fields of wild sugar cane. Soon she was used to the scent of burning sugar in the air.

Georgia was even starting
to look like an island girl.

But too soon Georgia's Hawaiian tour was over. It was now April and time for her to return home. From the deck of an elegant ocean liner, Georgia watched the green islands grow smaller and smaller until it was just her and the sea and the sky.

Georgia had created nearly twenty paintings of Hawaii. But she had not painted a pineapple.

Instead, she gave the Hawaiian Pineapple Company paintings of a heliconia flower and a papaya tree.

They were not happy. They wanted a pineapple!

Georgia was not happy either. She was not going to be told what to paint.

But then she thought about Hawaii and all that it had given her. She decided to give the company what they wanted.

Thirty-six hours later, a Hawaiian pineapple arrived at Georgia's penthouse in New York City—though Georgia didn't need it. When she closed her eyes, she could still see Hawaii and its sharp and beautiful fruit.

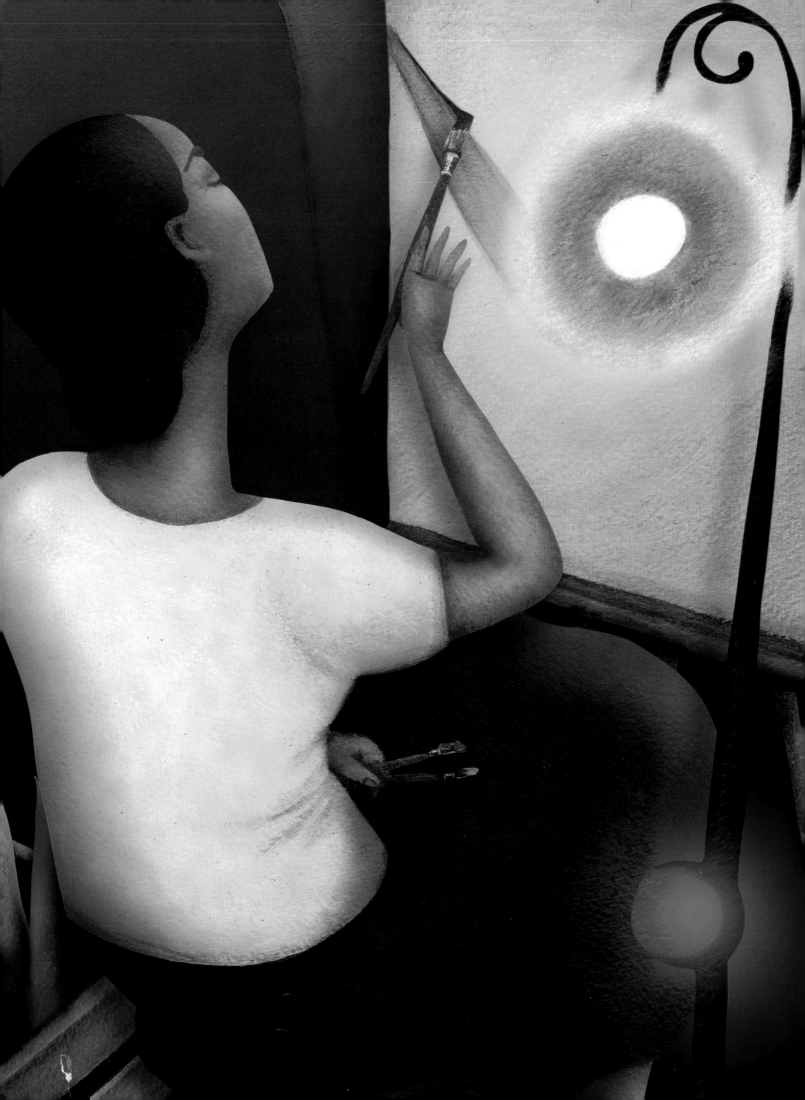

And Georgia painted a pineapple!

Author's Note

Georgia O'Keeffe was an American artist famous for her paintings of flowers when the Hawaiian Pineapple Company, later known as Dole, approached her to create two paintings for them.

At first, Georgia wasn't very excited to travel all the way to the middle of the Pacific Ocean. But once she began to study maps and pictures of Hawaii, she was eager to go.

Georgia took a train from her home in New York City across the country to San Francisco. There she climbed the gangplank of SS *Lurline* and sailed to the city of Honolulu on the island of Oahu.

The *Hilo Tribune Herald,* a local newspaper, announced her arrival with "Noted Woman Artist Arrives for Visit" (March 29, 1939), while the *Honolulu Advertiser* mentioned O'Keeffe's "hunter's green wool ensemble accented by crown flower leis and pink camellia blooms" (February 12, 1939).

Georgia loved Hawaii. She said that visiting there was one of the best things she ever did. Besides the pineapple incident, her one regret was that she didn't keep that rare piece of red coral she had found on the beach.

A year after returning home, Georgia showed twenty paintings of Hawaii, including her paintings of the heliconia flower and the pineapple, entitled *Pineapple Bud,* at a famous New York City gallery called An American Place, owned by her husband, Alfred Stieglitz. One reviewer from the *New York World-Telegram* wrote, "Her bird of paradise, her hibiscuses and her fish hooks silhouetted against the blue Hawaiian water are exciting and beautiful" (February 10, 1940).

And Georgia wrote, "If my painting is what I have to give back to the world for what the world has given to me . . . these paintings are what I have to give . . . for what three months in Hawaii gave to me."

For Further Reading

O'Keeffe, Georgia. *Georgia O'Keeffe.* New York: Viking Press, 1976.

Saville, Jennifer. *Georgia O'Keeffe: Paintings of Hawai'i.* Honolulu: Honolulu Academy of Arts, 1990.

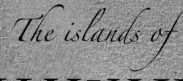

The islands of

HAWAII

Kauai

Niihau

Oahu

Molokai

Maui

Lanai

Hawaii

Kahoolawe

Pacific Ocean

Text copyright © 2012 by Amy Novesky
Illustrations copyright © 2012 by Yuyi Morales

Harcourt Children's Books is an imprint of Houghton Mifflin Harcourt Publishing Company.

www.hmhbooks.com

The illustrations in this book were done in acrylic on paper and then assembled digitally.
The text type was set in Wade Sans Light.
The display type was set in Avenida Std.
Design by Regina Roff

Library of Congress Cataloging-in-Publication Data
Novesky, Amy.
Georgia in Hawaii : when Georgia O'Keeffe painted what she pleased /
written by Amy Novesky ; illustrated by Yuyi Morales.
p. cm.
Summary: In 1939, artist Georgia O'Keeffe creates nearly twenty
paintings as she tours the Hawaiian islands, but refuses to paint
pictures of pineapples the way her sponsors tell her to.
ISBN 978-0-15-205420-5
1. O'Keeffe, Georgia, 1887-1986—Juvenile fiction. [1. O'Keeffe, Georgia,
1887-1986—Fiction. 2. Painting—Fiction. 3. Artists—Fiction.
4. Obstinacy—Fiction. 5. Hawaii—History—
1900-1959—Fiction.]
1. Morales, Yuyi, ill. II. Title.
PZ7.N869Geo 2012
[E]—dc22
2010043401

Manufactured in Malaysia
TWP 10 9 8 7 6 5 4 3 2 1
4500468326

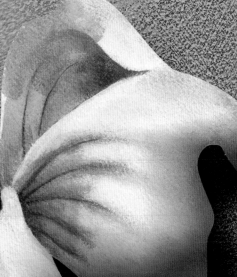

ILLUSTRATOR'S NOTE

While creating the illustrations for this book, I looked carefully at Georgia O'Keeffe's artwork. How wonderful to imagine her fascination at looking deep into a flower, her delight in finding a rare piece of coral, and her surprise at discovering magic in a fishhook! Art is a collaboration between the artist and the viewer. What do you imagine when you look at Georgia's paintings?

I decided to interpret not only the twenty paintings Georgia created about Hawaii, but also other elements from paintings she made during her long career. In the story, Georgia's streak of frustration at being told what to paint is depicted through a sharp form influenced by her painting *Orange and Red Streak*, 1919. A glowing volcano on the big island of Hawaii takes shape with inspiration from *Special No. 21 (Palo Duro Canyon)*, 1916. The walls of her New York studio come alive with buildings, the moon, and a streetlight reminiscent of her *New York with Moon*, 1925.

I illustrated these and other elements inspired by her artwork because this is how I imagine Georgia expressing her emotions—through her paintings. I hope these details give readers an opportunity to create their own narrative, to see themselves reflected in this artist's work, and to experience unique discoveries and delights about Georgia's time in Hawaii, where she painted more than just a pineapple.

A Special Thanks

Ever since we were kids, my siblings and I have spent time daydreaming and putting our creative sparks together. In this book we have done it once again. My sister Magaly brought her painting skills to this story. My brother, Mario Alejandro, brought his digital magic to help me clean and assemble the many elements of this book. I thank them for helping me create art that's even more special to me than the work I do alone. —Y.M.

SILVER CUP

PLUMERIA

HELICONIA

BIRD OF PARADISE